THE STORY OF
VENUS AND TANNHÄUSER
OR "UNDER THE HILL"

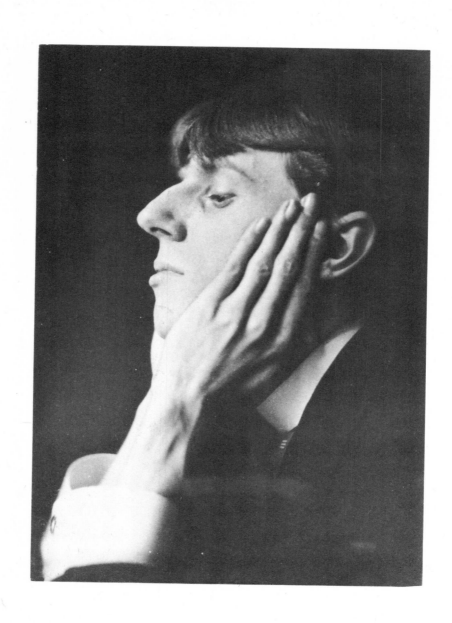

THE STORY OF
VENUS AND TANNHÄUSER
OR "UNDER THE HILL"

in which is set forth an exact account
of the manner of state held by
Madam Venus, Goddess and Meretrix,
under the famous Hörselberg, and
containing the Adventures of
Tannhäuser in that place, his
Repentance, his Journeying to Rome
and Return to the Loving Mountain.

A ROMANTIC NOVEL
BY
AUBREY BEARDSLEY

with twelve illustrations from the
author's own hand and two
illustrations from photographs

edited with an introduction
by
ROBERT ORESKO

ACADEMY EDITIONS · LONDON/ST · MARTIN'S PRESS · NEW YORK

Frontispiece
Aubrey Beardsley, a photograph taken by his friend Frederick H. Evans.
Evans owned a bookshop which Beardsley often visited, and it was on his recommenda-
tion that in 1892 John Dent commissioned Beardsley to illustrate a new edition of Sir
Thomas Malory's *Le Morte Darthur*, the young man's first undertaking as a professional
artist. Evans also collected several Beardsley drawings.

Published in Great Britain by Academy Editions
7 Holland Street   London   W8

SBN 85670 167 X cloth   SBN 85670 172 6 paper

Copyright © Academy Editions 1974. All rights reserved

Published in the U.S.A. in 1974 by St. Martin's Press Inc.
175 Fifth Avenue   New York   N.Y. 10010

Library of Congress Catalog Number 74–78463

Text set in Monotype Bembo,
printed by photolithography, and bound in Great Britain
at The Pitman Press, Bath

EDITOR'S NOTE

As discussed in the introduction, this current edition of Aubrey Beardsley's *Story of Venus and Tannhäuser* is based, with two exceptions, upon the 1907 version of the tale as printed privately by Leonard Smithers. Both exceptions appear in chapter seven and are two passages which have been interpolated into the Smithers text from the second number of *The Savoy* (April 1896). The first runs from the line beginning "He thought of the 'Romaunt de la Rose'" to that ending with "upon the rose striped walls." This extensive section replaces the following brief passage from the 1907 version: " 'and what delightful pictures,' he continued, wandering his eyes from print to print that hung upon the rose striped walls." This first interpolation contains three footnotes including a sizeable one devoted to a description of Sporion's bacchanale. As this description appears largely unaltered as part of chapter five in the Smithers version, and hence also in this edition, footnote no. 3 has been limited to the first two sentences of the corresponding footnote in *The Savoy* text.

The second interpolation, beginning with the words "Tannhäuser had taken some books" and ending with "splendid agitation of it all!," has simply been inserted between two paragraphs in the 1907 text, displacing none of the Smithers version.

In both *Savoy* passages the names of "the Abbé," "Fanfreluche" and "Helen" have been altered to "the Chevalier," "Tannhäuser" and "Venus" respectively. Obvious and misleading typographical errors in both spelling and punctuation have been corrected.

Aubrey Beardsley in the room of the Hôtel Cosmopolitain, Menton, France, where he died.
Three of the photographs on the bookcase are identifiable as those of Mabel Beardsley, the beloved sister with whom Beardsley may have had an incestuous relationship, of André Raffalovich, the patron who was instrumental in converting Beardsley to Catholicism, and, of Wagner, another nineteenth century interpreter of the Tannhäuser legend.

INTRODUCTION

1895 was a year of disasters for Aubrey Vincent Beardsley. The conviction of Oscar Wilde for homosexual offences initiated an intensely paranoid reaction against the so-called "Decadent" school of writers and artists, of which Beardsley, whom Wilde had dubbed a "monstrous orchid," was one of the most successful and best known members. Although Beardsley's relations with Wilde were by this time strained and bitter, and even though Beardsley was probably not homosexual, he was, nevertheless, closely associated in the public mind with Wilde, Lord Alfred Douglas and their set. He had, after all, provided a series of stunning illustrations for "Salome," which Lord Alfred had translated into English from Wilde's French, and at least at the beginning of his career, Beardsley and his drawings had found favour in the Wilde circle. For such guardians of public morality as Alice Meynel and Mrs. Humphrey Ward this was enough to taint Beardsley with the lavender brush of homosexuality, and John Lane was forced to dismiss him from his post as art editor of *The Yellow Book*, the leading "Decadent" journal in Britain. Beardsley's problems were only aggravated by the deterioration of his health, which had been totally undermined by tuberculosis, and at the age of twenty-three he began to realise that he was a dying man. By the next year he could see "no end to the chapter of blood."

Some respite from his difficulties was offered by Leonard Smithers, a lawyer and a publisher of erotic literature, who asked Beardsley to join the staff of his new periodical, *The Savoy*. The first number of *The Savoy* appeared in January 1896, with Beardsley as artistic editor, both advising on the contributions of other draughtsmen and providing drawings of his own for the new venture. But besides his decorations and sketches, the debut issue of *The Savoy* also contained one of Beardsley's infrequent literary efforts, the first three chapters of a "romantic story" published under the title "Under the Hill," with three illustrations by the author. This was the beginning of *The Story of Venus and Tannhäuser*. The original Tannhäuser was a minstrel, living in the early thirteenth century, during the decline of the medieval minnesänger tradition. This historical figure merged into that of the legendary knight, who, as the lover of Frau Hulda, the German folklorist equivalent of Venus, visited the Hörselberg, or Venusberg, the embodiment of carnality in the Gothic world. Through the intervention of the Virgin, the chevalier Tannhäuser repented of his sensual excesses and left the Venusberg to seek Pope Urban's forgiveness in Rome. This pilgrimage ended in frustration, for the Pope proclaimed that the knight's sins were so great that it would be as likely for the episcopal staff to sprout leaves as for him to receive mercy. Tannhäuser instantly returned to the Venusberg, and, three days later, when the staff miraculously burgeoned forth, none of the papal messengers sent out to bring the disappointed penitent back to Rome could find him.

Beardsley had been intrigued by the literary possibilities of the Tannhäuser legend for some time, and in 1894 John Lane announced the future publication of "*The Story of Venus and Tannhäuser . . .* by Aubrey

Beardsley. With twenty full-page illustrations, numerous ornaments and a cover from the same hand." Rather optimistically, Beardsley included a copy of the proposed *Story of Venus and Tannhäuser*, along with volumes of Dickens and Shakespeare, in an unused design for the front cover of *The Yellow Book*. Neither this project nor a similar one planned by H. Henry & Co. Ltd. ever came to fruition, although Beardsley executed at least four drawings relating to the Tannhäuser story for these unrealised ventures, including one, "Venus between Terminal Gods," which won the admiration of Lord Leighton. Finally, in 1896, parts of Beardsley's text began to appear in *The Savoy*. Although the events of "Under the Hill" and *The Story of Venus and Tannhäuser* are remarkably similar—indeed paragraph after paragraph are identical—there are some important differences between the surviving Beardsley manuscript and its form as published in *The Savoy*. Apart from some incidental alteration of words and phrases, the names of the chief protagonists were changed for *The Savoy* serialisation. Tannhäuser emerges with the exotic tag of the Abbé Fanfreluche, while, somewhat more understandably, Venus is metamorphosed into Helen. More importantly, however, Smithers and his literary editor, Arthur Symons, purged Beardsley's text of erotic allusions and descriptions which might have offended the tender sensitivities of a London still shocked by the revelations of the Wilde trials. *The Savoy*, in short, offered its readers only three chapters of bowdlerised Beardsley, with three new illustrations. Obviously Symons envisioned publishing the entire, albeit "purified" text of "Under the Hill" as a serial—Beardsley wrote it piecemeal—in *The Savoy*, and the second number, of April 1896, contained chapter four of the romantic fable. Again, the text was censored, and Beardsley contributed two further illustrations, but at the end of the magazine Smithers felt compelled to inform his subscribers "that owing to Mr. Beardsley's illness he has been unable to finish one of his full-page drawings to Chapter IV of 'Under the Hill,' i.e. 'The Bacchanals of Sporion,' and that its publication in consequence has had to be postponed to No. 3 of *The Savoy*." The third number appeared in July 1896 without any additional text to "Under the Hill" and without the promised plate of "The Bacchanals of Sporion." Again, Smithers offered an apology and ominously explained that "In consequence of Mr. Beardsley's severe and continued illness, we have been compelled to discontinue the publication of 'Under the Hill', which will be issued by the present publisher in book form, with numerous illustrations by the author, as soon as Mr. Beardsley is well enough to carry on the work to its conclusion."

By April of 1896 Beardsley's health was in shambles; in his own words, he had "stained many a fair handkerchief with blood." The exertions of his life in London merely undermined him further, and by the summer, after consulting a specialist, Beardsley had become "really depressed and frightened about myself." Finally, in the spring of 1897, he left the damp English climate for the more temperate one of France, spending his time in Paris and Dieppe. By November 1897, Beardsley was so weakened that his physicians urged him to move even further south, and, accompanied by his mother, he went to Menton. Throughout this entire period Beardsley continued to draw unreservedly upon his quickly diminishing resources of energy, and he completed both individual sketches for *The Savoy* and his famous illustrations for Aristophanes's "Lysistrata." He also began his drawings for Ben Jonson's "Volpone," but despite assurances to Smithers in April and June 1896 that he was continuing work on "Under the Hill" he seems to have found little time for his literary effort. At Beardsley's death, at the age of twenty-five, on 16 March 1898, his romantic tale was still unfinished.

At first glance the legacy of Beardsley's interest in the Tannhäuser legend may seem scant. It consists of ten illustrations, one early, amateurish effort which ultimately served as the basis for "The Return of Tannhäuser," four completed for the early unrealised projects of John Lane and H. Henry and five included in the two *Savoy* instalments. There are also two sets of Beardsley text: the unexpurgated manuscript version in ten chapters which leaves Tannhäuser, restored to his real name, still enjoying the delights of the Venusberg and seemingly quite far from repentance, and the heavily censored "Under the Hill" of *The Savoy* serialisation. In 1904 John Lane republished "Under the Hill" in a collection of Beardsley's occasional writings. This slim volume included the five illustrations which Beardsley drew for *The Savoy* instalments but, as expected, also observed the deletions made for the sake of Edwardian decency. It was not until 1907 that the original manuscript, which Beardsley had sent bit by bit to Smithers, saw light of day, and then only in a limited and private edition of three hundred copies. Although this version opened up all the cuts which his publisher had imposed, it did not include Beardsley's illustrations. For some reason, it also eliminated two passages from chapter seven, "How Tannhäuser awakened and took his morning ablutions in the Venusberg." These two sections appeared in chapter four of *The Savoy* instalments, and, besides their charm and wit, they are important because they justify the presence of two illustrations, "St. Rose of Lima" and "Das Rheingold," which otherwise would seem to have no relationship to Beardsley's text. The Smithers version was printed a second time, in New York in 1927, again privately and again without the two innocuous but necessary passages from *The Savoy* text. This volume was, however, illustrated not with Beardsley's work but with the decidedly more commonplace designs of Bertram Elliott. Finally, in 1959, Olympia Press brought out its own version of *The Story of Venus and Tannhäuser*. This edition included Beardsley's original illustrations, but in addition to restoring the missing passages in chapter seven, it also departed from the Smithers version in other, sometimes minor but often inexplicable, ways. Moreover, the Olympia version was "completed" by John Glassco, and however interesting this addition may be in its own right, its decidedly modern jargon cannot fail but set it apart as an anachronistic appendage grafted onto the unfinished work of a master. We shall, of course, never know precisely how Beardsley planned to present *The Story of Venus and Tannhäuser* had he lived to complete it, but the present edition hopes to assemble into a coherent whole all of the material Beardsley produced for this project. We have used the 1907 Smithers version of the text as the basis for this new edition, but to this we have added all of Beardsley's Tannhäuser illustrations, which according to the pre-publication release he had intended to include in the complete book, and we have also restored the two passages recounting Tannhäuser's musings in bed after Sporion's bacchanale. As stated above, those sections, which appeared in *The Savoy* but are not in the Smithers version, easily fit into the 1907 edition and are essential if two of Beardsley's drawings are to make any sense within the context of *The Story of Venus and Tannhäuser*. Accordingly, these passages are included in this new edition, although an editor's note explains precisely where these alterations in the Smithers text occur.

In light of the relatively liberated moral and artistic standards of the late twentieth century it is occasionally difficult to understand why Beardsley's *Story of Venus and Tannhäuser* is not better known and more widely valued than it is today. Surely "the freedom of certain passages," to use Smither's felicitous phrase, is less shocking now than it might have been eighty years ago, and this "romantic story" is undeniably unique in the oeuvre of a man whose skill, originality and importance have attracted increasing appreciation and scholarly attention during the past ten years. *The Story of Venus and Tannhäuser* was Beardsley's attempt to create a total work of art, an almost Wagnerian conception of the individual artist controlling every means of expression—in this case, the literary and the graphic—of a given theme. Apart from his letters, some occasional poetry and aphoristic table talk, pallid reflections of Wilde, *The Story of Venus and Tannhäuser* is Beardsley's only literary effort, and even if it were not as sparkling and graceful as it is, this romantic fantasy would still hold interest for the light it sheds upon the mind of one of England's most remarkable "Decadent" artists. Although Beardsley's reputation and fame rest solidly upon his achievement as an illustrator, there are indications that he aimed ultimately for a career as a writer, or at least at one which would draw upon both his literary and graphic talents. Arthur Symons, one of Beardsley's close friends, a colleague and a perceptive critic, paid tribute to the artist's "undoubted, singular, literary ability." He added that "I think Beardsley would rather have been a great writer than a great artist; and I can remember, on one occasion, when he had to fill up a form of admission to some library to which I was introducing him, his insistence on describing himself as a 'man of letters.'" Symons concluded that "Beardsley was very anxious to be a writer."

Certainly, much of Beardsley's graphic oeuvre has a decidedly literary aspect, for apart from the fact that many of his drawings were commissioned to illustrate the works of great writers, Beardsley's designs were often crammed with literary allusions. His "Toilet of Salome," for instance, includes a bookcase with copies of Apulius's *The Golden Ass*, Zola's *Nana*, Prévost's *Manon Lescaut*, Verlaine's *Les Fêtes Galantes* and the works of the marquis de Sade. These books have obvious connections to Beardsley's view of Wilde's princess of Judea, but they also underline the artist's own literary preoccupation and interests.

This technique of scattering references to his favourite books throughout his own work is characteristic of Beardsley and often extended to an identical manipulation of musical allusions. From his childhood, Beardsley had been passionately fond of music, and this interest bore fruit in his caricatures of Weber, Chopin, Mendelssohn and Paganini. Indeed, in his Tannhäuser story, Beardsley deployed musical allusions with an ease fully comparable to that with which he sprinkled the inevitable literary references throughout his work. In the last chapter, for instance, the lovers hear a performance of Rossini's Stabat Mater, complete with a male alto. The most obvious musical inspiration for Beardsley's tale, however, was Wagner's "Tannhäuser," which was first performed in Dresden in 1845, a revised version being premiered in Paris in 1861. Beardsley had always been a fervent admirer of the German master, and throughout his career the young Englishman drew upon Wagner's oeuvre and his cult for some of his most celebrated compositions, most notably "The Wagnerites." Beardsley also portrayed Max Alvary and Katerina Klavski in their costumes as Tristan and Isolde, and "Der Ring des Nibelungen" provided an especially fecund source book for Beardsley's genius: Erda, Loge, Siegfried and Flosshilde all figure in his work. There are especially pronounced Wagnerian elements in Beardsley's recounting of the story of Tannhäuser. The chevalier, for instance, flips through the score of "Das Rheingold" the morning after the bacchanale. Beardsley also included a full page illustration for this episode, his own rendering of the third tableau from "Das Rheingold," the crucial scene in which Wotan and Loge cheat the transformed Nibelung, Alberich, of the gold he has purloined from the Rheinmädchen. In addition, Beardsley made a passing reference to a photograph of the great French baritone Victor Maurel, as Wolfram von Eschenbach. There is a direct link here, as Maurel sang Wolfram in the first London production of "Tannhäuser" at Covent Garden on 6 May 1876. But despite Beardsley's affection for and knowledge of the Wagnerian canon, his own version of Tannhäuser was apparently meant to develop quite differently from Wagner's. Wagner had married the Tannhäuser legend, as embodied in the minnesänger tradition and in Ludwig Tieck's *Der getreue Eckart und der Tannhäuser*, to the accounts of the *sangkrieg* or minstrels's war found in Grimm's *Sagen*. As far as can be determined from the preface and full title of *The Story of Venus and Tannhäuser*, Beardsley had no intention of including the song contest at the Wartburg for the hand of the pure Elisabeth in his own account of this medieval legend. Indeed, although his tone was very different, at least in terms of plot development, Beardsley seems to have envisioned a return to the old German tale of a knight who visits the Venusberg, repents of his unbridled indulgences in sensuality, but disappears after a papal refusal of forgiveness.

Despite these occasional Wagnerian motifs and the Teutonic origins of the Tannhäuser legend itself, Beardsley's narration most definitely belongs not to the Gothic north but to the Catholic south. Beardsley's muse was a Gallic one. As Robert Ross, who met him in 1892, remarked, "He was full of Molière and *Manon Lescaut*." The predominant French flavour is apparent in the first few pages of *The Story of Venus and Tannhäuser*, and the entire text is riddled with French words and phrases, usually dispersed without distinguishing italics. The epigraph is a quotation from the *Roman de la Rose*, the thirteenth century poetic celebration of love, both sacred and profane, which, with its gently veiled vocabulary of anatomical detail, must have served as a prototype for Beardsley's description of Venus's erotic festivities. Perhaps even more influential as a literary pattern for Beardsley's account were the *Moralités légendaires* of Jules Laforgue, who, in a grimly coincidental irony, died of tuberculosis in 1887 at the age of twenty-seven. The *Moralités légendaires* consist of six satirical elaborations upon such half-mythic figures as Salome, Lohengrin and Hamlet, and Beardsley's more than occasional irreverence towards Tannhäuser's diversions at Venus's court owe Laforgue's charming conceits a large debt.

In many ways, Beardsley's *Story of Venus and Tannhäuser* is a belated child of the French rococo. According to Brian Reade's analysis, one of the manifestations of Beardsley's reaction to his fall from favour after the Wilde trials was a withdrawal into the rococo: "his art took a fresh turn, this time away from the world he saw around him and towards an imagined world of the eighteenth century, based on the ideal art of that century, from Watteau to the *petit maîtres* of the *ancien régime*." Beardsley's newly articulated delight in the rococo found its most complete expression in his designs for Alexander Pope's *The Rape of the Lock*. But Beardsley's text for *The Story of Venus and Tann-*

häuser is also permeated with the gentle cynicism and muted erotic titillation so common in the *contes amoureuses* of the eighteenth century. To Edmund Wilson, it was the figure of the flirtatious Venus which epitomised this rococo element in Beardsley's tale. She has much more of Manon or one of Marivaux's heroines than she does of the depraved Salome, and, as Wilson observed, Venus "really approaches much nearer to the naive naughtiness of the eighteenth century than anything to be found in Wilde . . . a neo-eighteenth century world, erotic, light-hearted and skeptical . . . ." If Beardsley drew upon the literature of the classical, medieval and nineteenth century worlds for specific attitudes and episodes in *The Story of Venus and Tannhäuser*, the charm, civilised detachment, fastidious concern with small amenities, cultivated eroticism and total lack of moral didacticism place this romantic story firmly in the *ancien régime*, or at least, in the sybaritic world of the court *noblesse* and urban *haute bourgeoisie* which Beardsley had read of in novels and had come to think of as representative of the entire eighteenth century.

In some ways, Beardsley used *The Story of Venus and Tannhäuser* as a setting for the display of a range of knowledge, which, in its staggering richness of unfocused and disorganised arcana, occasionally displayed with a touch of preciosity, bore all the earmarks of the auto-didact. Certainly Beardsley made no effort to conceal the sources of inspiration for his literary work, and the varied references and allusions to the works of earlier masters provide an eloquent tribute to both his wide reading and his intellectual curiosity, even though his occasionally self-conscious manipulation of these sources betrays equally clearly the hand of a man resolutely bent upon "self-improvement." Robert Ross commented on Beardsley's intellectual eagerness, reminiscing that "his knowledge of Balzac astonished an authority on the subject who was present. He spoke much of the National Gallery and the British Museum, both of which he knew with extraordinary thoroughness." Beardsley's rummagings through French and German culture have been discussed above, but he obviously drew inspiration from wherever he could find it. The bacchanale seems to owe some debt, if only in its extravagance, to the Cena Trimalchionis from the *Satyricon* of Petronius, while Tannhäuser's fleeting pederastic diversion in the bath was directly inspired by an identical episode in Suetonius's account of the Emperor

Tiberius. Even that rich source book for Renaissance iconography, Francesco Colonna's *Hypnerotomachia Poliphili*, published in the famous Manutius edition of 1499 and re-issued in a facsimile version in 1889, left its traces, most obviously in the composite columns and architectural framework of the frontispiece and title page which Beardsley designed in 1894.

What spares this display of erudition in Beardsley's narrative from the accusation of pedantry is the deft lightness with which it is worn. Fact and fantasy mingle freely in *The Story of Venus and Tannhäuser*. References to the Carmontelle drawing of the eighteenth century *salonnière* Mme du Deffand, to Molière's famous curved moustaches and the historically verifiable sexual excesses of the Regent Orléans alternate with such witty fabrications as *A Plea for the Domestication of the Unicorn*, which Tannhäuser finds in Venus's library, and the tenth chapter of Pénillière's history of underlinen. Beardsley introduced the figure of the seventeenth century Latin American St. Rose of Lima, only to launch into totally whimsical speculations upon the wisdom of a four year old girl vowing herself to perpetual chastity. But perhaps Beardsley's most elaborate, and hence, triumphant conceit is the prefatory epistle (an art form which "has fallen into disuse, whether through the vanity of authors or the humility of patrons") dedicated to the fictitious Cardinal Giulio Poldo Pezzoli, who held such colourful posts as those of titular bishop of S. Maria in Trastavere, archbishop of Ostia and Valletri and papal nuncio in Nicaragua and Patagonia.

From time to time this cultivated playfulness could assume a rather sharpened, acerbic edge, as in the brutal portrait of Wilde, both in the text and in "The Toilet of Venus," as the love goddess's monstrous and bloated attendant, Priapusa. But it is the tone and ambiance of lightness which predominates, which connects the story spiritually to the French rococo and which endows the erotic diversions at the Venusberg with the aura of both good humour and an almost over-refined delicacy. The highly sophisticated wit and charm of *The Story of Venus and Tannhäuser* are as far removed from the dreary and mirthless pornography of the contemporary scene as they are from the descriptions of the straightforward sexual excitements experienced by Daniel Defoe's Moll Flanders and John Cleland's Fanny Hill some two hundred years earlier. As Paul Gillette wrote, "Beardsley reverts to the climate of ancient Greek and Roman erotica, a climate wherein sex is viewed as good-clean-fun, indulgence in it as taken as a matter of course and descriptions of sexual liaisons concentrate less upon the mechanics of acts performed than upon the atmosphere in which they were performed."

Beardsley always managed to make his point without ever being explicit. Indeed, he almost assembled his own vocabulary of sexuality based upon a gently ironic sense of humour rather than a profusion of erotic detail. The exact significance of the "five finger exercise," of Venus lapping "her little aperitif" and of Tannhäuser's "panting blade" will not be lost on anyone with the slightest imagination. The more exotic and rarefied anal delights of taking one's coffee "aux deux colonnes" and "licking the paint off" "petits couillons" and "petits derrières" may be more hidden, but the very point of *The Story of Venus and Tannhäuser*, and indeed, of Beardsley's entire oeuvre, is that sex is part of a style not the style itself. Eroticism had for Beardsley an almost oxymoron existence of being at once necessary and at the same time not important enough to treat seriously. Any retelling of the Tannhäuser legend must contain some carnality if the Pope's refusal to grant the chevalier forgiveness in Rome is to have any plausibility at all. Beardsley's Venusberg is an entire, enclosed world in and of itself, and sex happens to play an integral role in this society, but by managing to treat Venus's court with a mildly frivolous, civilised and detached attitude, he avoided the unrelieved dreariness of both a preachy morality tale and a catalogue of erotic indulgence. Beardsley's narrative is, in this way, a late nineteenth century instalment of the Graeco-Roman and rococo comic traditions, in which sex was presented with humour and lightness but not permitted to dominate the entire proceedings.

From one point of view, Beardsley's unfinished *Story of Venus and Tannhäuser* may seem to have a greater erotic orientation than the author had intended. Obviously, we shall never know what Beardsley planned for the development and culmination of his narrative, but it is clear that no matter how much he was enjoying writing about life at the Venusberg, sooner or later Beardsley would have had to have moved his hero to Rome. A convert to Roman Catholicism, Beardsley was as addicted to ceremonial minutiae as he was to the sartorial and theatrical niceties at the Venusberg, and, although this can only be speculation, it seems more than likely that the sections dealing with Tannhäuser's penitence and his visit to Rome might have balanced the extravagances of Venus's courtiers.

From Michelangelo's Captives to Puccini's "Turandot," it has always proved difficult to assess fairly a masterpiece left incomplete. As with Aubrey Beardsley's *Story of Venus and Tannhäuser*, it is impossible to know how the narrative would have proceeded or even what revisions and alterations the author might have made of that part of the manuscript which we are fortunate enough to possess. But it is certain that, in the words of Stanley Weintraub, "However unfinished and fragmentary, the combination of pictures and prose" for *The Story of Venus and Tannhäuser* "represents one of the great creative achievements of the period." It is not only an essential document for understanding the vision of one of England's outstanding "Decadent" artists but also a remarkable contribution to the rich European tradition of the Tannhäuser legend, stretching from the early thirteenth century as a legacy of the minnesänger. It is hoped that this new edition of *The Story of Venus and Tannhäuser*, which for the first time assembles all of Beardsley's work, both literary and graphic, on the Tannhäuser tradition, in its original form, will bring this neglected, albeit, unfinished masterpiece the appreciation and acclaim which it deserves.

Title page and frontispiece
from the original drawing by Aubrey Beardsley now at the Fogg Art Museum, Harvard University, Cambridge, Massachusetts, U.S.A.
reproduced as pl. 92 in *The Early Work of Aubrey Beardsley*.

THE STORY OF VENUS
AND TANNHÄUSER, IN
WHICH IS SET FORTH AN
EXACT ACCOUNT OF THE
MANNER OF STATE HELD
BY MADAM VENUS, GOD-
DESS AND MERETRIX,
UNDER THE FAMOUS
HÖRSELBERG, AND CON-
TAINING THE ADVEN-
TURES OF TANNHÄUSER
IN THAT PLACE, HIS RE-
PENTANCE, HIS JOURNEY-
ING TO ROME, AND RE-
TURN TO THE LOVING
MOUNTAIN. By AUBREY
BEARDSLEY. &&&&&&

"La chaleur du brandon Vénus"

Le Roman de la Rose, v. 22051

TO
THE MOST EMINENT AND REVEREND PRINCE
GIULIO POLDO PEZZOLI
CARDINAL OF THE HOLY ROMAN CHURCH
TITULAR BISHOP OF S. MARIA IN TRASTAVERE
ARCHBISHOP OF OSTIA AND VELLETRI
NUNCIO TO THE HOLY SEE
IN
NICARAGUA AND PATAGONIA
A FATHER TO THE POOR
A REFORMER OF ECCLESIASTICAL DISCIPLINE
A PATTERN OF LEARNING
WISDOM AND HOLINESS OF LIFE
THIS BOOK IS DEDICATED WITH DUE REVERENCE
BY HIS HUMBLE SERVITOR
A SCRIVENER AND LIMNER OF WORLDLY THINGS
WHO MADE THIS BOOK
AUBREY BEARDSLEY

MOST EMINENT PRINCE, I know not by what mischance the writing of epistles dedicatory has fallen into disuse, whether through the vanity of authors or the humility of patrons. But the practice seems to me so very beautiful and becoming that I have ventured to make an essay in the modest art, and lay with formalities my first book at your feet. I have, it must be confessed, many fears lest I shall be arraigned of presumption in choosing so exalted a name as your own to place at the beginning of these histories; but I hope that such a censure will not be too lightly passed upon me, for, if I am guilty, 'tis but of a most natural pride that the accidents of my life should allow me to sail the little pinnace of my wit under your protection.

But though I can clear myself of such a charge, I am still minded to use the tongue of apology, for with what face can I offer you a book treating of so vain and fantastical a thing as Love? I know that in the judgment of many the amorous passion is accounted a shameful thing and ridiculous; indeed, it must be confessed that more blushes have risen for Love's sake than for any other cause, and that lovers are an eternal laughing-stock. Still, as the book will be found to contain matter of deeper import than mere venery, inasmuch as it treats of the great contrition of its chiefest character, and of canonical things in its chapters, I am not without hopes that your Eminence will pardon my writing of the Hill of Venus, for which exposition let my youth excuse me.

Then I must crave your forgiveness for addressing you in a language other than the Roman, but my small freedom in Latinity forbids me to wander beyond the idiom of my vernacular. I would not for the world that your delicate Southern ear should be offended by a barbarous assault of rude and Gothic words; but methinks no language is rude that can boast polite writers, and not a few have flourished in this country in times past, bringing our common speech to very great perfection. In the present age, alas! our pens are ravished by unlettered authors and unmannered critics, that make a havoc rather than a building, a wilderness rather than a garden. But, alack! what boots it to drop tears upon the preterit?

'Tis not of our own shortcomings, though, but of your own great merits that I should speak, else I should be forgetful of the duties I have drawn upon myself in electing to address you in a dedication. 'Tis of your noble virtues (though all the world know of 'em), your taste and wit, your care for letters, and very real regard for the arts, that I must be the proclaimer.

Though it be true that all men have sufficient wit to a pass a judgment on this or that, and not a few sufficient impudence to print the same (these being commonly accounted critics), I have ever held that the critical faculty is more rare than the inventive. 'Tis a faculty your Eminence possesses in so great a degree that your praise or blame is something oracular, your utterance infallible as great genius or as a beautiful woman. Your mind, I know, rejoicing in fine distinctions and subtle procedures of thought, beautifully discursive rather than hastily conclusive, has found in criticism its happiest exercise. 'Tis pity that so perfect a Mecænas should have no Horace to befriend, no Georgics to accept; for the offices and function of patron or critic must of necessity be lessened in an age of little men and little work. In times past 'twas nothing derogatory for great princes and men of State to extend their loves and favour to poets, for thereby they received as much honour as they conferred. Did not Prince Festus with pride take the master-work of Julian into his protection, and was not the Æneid a pretty thing to offer Cæsar?

Learning without appreciation is a thing of nought, but I know not which is greatest in you, your love of the arts or your knowledge of 'em. What wonder, then, that I am studious to please you, and desirous of your protection? How deeply thankful I am for your past affections, you know well, your great kindness and liberality having far outgone my slight merits and small accomplishment that seemed scarce to warrant any favour. Alas! 'tis a slight offering I make you now, but, if after glancing into its pages (say of an evening upon your terrace), you should deem it worthy of the most remote place in your princely library, the knowledge that it rested there would be reward sufficient for my labours, and a crowning happiness to my pleasure in the writing of this slender book.

The humble and obedient servant of your Eminence,

AUBREY BEARDSLEY.

The Chevalier Tannhäuser (also called "The Abbé")
original drawing ($9\frac{13}{16} \times 6\frac{7}{8}$ in.) in the collection of Mr. R. A. Harari, London
reproduced on p. 157 in *The Savoy*, no. 1 (January 1896), on p. 9 in *Under the Hill* (London, 1904) and as pl. 120 in *The Later Work of Aubrey Beardsley*.

CHAPTER I

HOW THE CHEVALIER TANNHÄUSER ENTERED INTO THE HILL OF VENUS.

The Chevalier Tannhäuser, having lighted off his horse, stood doubtfully for a moment beneath the ombre gateway of the Venusberg, troubled with an exquisite fear lest a day's travel should have too cruelly undone the laboured niceness of his dress. His hand, slim and gracious as La Marquise du Deffand's in the drawing by Carmontelle, played nervously about the gold hair that fell upon his shoulders like a finely curled peruke, and from point to point of a precise toilet, the fingers wandered, quelling the little mutinies of cravat and ruffle.

It was taper-time; when the tired earth puts on its cloak of mists and shadows, when the enchanted woods are stirred with light footfalls and slender voices of the fairies, when all the air is full of delicate influences, and even the beaux, seated at their dressing-tables, dream a little.

A delicious moment, thought Tannhäuser, to slip into exile.

The place where he stood waved drowsily with strange flowers, heavy with perfume, dripping with odours. Gloomy and nameless weeds not to be found in Mentzelius. Huge moths so richly winged they must have banqueted upon tapestries and royal stuffs, slept on the pillars that flanked either side of the gateway, and the eyes of all the moths remained open, and were burning and bursting with a mesh of veins. The pillars were fashioned in some pale stone, and rose up like hymns in the praise of Venus, for, from cap to base, each one was carved with loving sculptures, showing such a cunning invention and such a curious knowledge that Tannhäuser lingered not a little in reviewing them. They surpassed all that Japan has ever pictured from her maisons vertes, all that was ever painted on the pretty bathrooms of Cardinal La Motte, and even outdid the astonishing illustration to Jones' *"Nursery Numbers."*

"A pretty portal," murmured the Chevalier, correcting his sash.

As he spake, a faint sound of singing was breathed out from the mountain, faint music as strange and distant as sea-legends that are heard in shells.

"The Vespers of Venus, I take it," said Tannhäuser and struck a few chords of accompaniment ever so lightly upon his little lute. Softly across the spell-bound threshold the song floated and wreathed itself about the subtle columns till the moths were touched with passion, and moved quaintly in their sleep. One of them was awakened by the intenser notes of the Chevalier's lute-strings, and fluttered into his cave. Tannhäuser felt it was his cue for entry.

"Adieu," he exclaimed, with an inclusive gesture, and "Good-bye, Madonna" as the cold circle of the moon began to show, beautiful and full of enchantments. There was a shadow of sentiment in his voice as he spake the words.

"Would to heaven," he sighed, "I might receive the assurance of a looking-glass before I make my début! However, as she is a goddess, I doubt not her eyes are a little sated with perfection, and may not be displeased to see it crowned with a tiny fault."

A wild rose had caught upon the trimmings of his muff, and in the first flush of displeasure he would have struck it brusquely away, and most severely punished the offending flower. But the ruffled mood lasted only a moment, for there was something so deliciously incongruous in the hardy petal's invasion of so delicate a thing, that Tannhäuser withheld the finger of resentment, and vowed that the wild rose should stay where it had clung—a passport, as it were, from the upper to the underworld.

"The very excess and violence of the fault," he said, "will be its excuse;" and, undoing a tangle in the tassel of his stick, stepped into the shadowy corridor that ran into the bosom of the wan hill, stepped with the admirable aplomb and unwrinkled suavity of Don John.

The Toilet of Venus (also called "The Toilet" and "The Toilet of Helen") reproduced on p. 161 in *The Savoy*, no. 1 (January 1896), on p. 13 in *Under the Hill* (London, 1904) and as pl. 121 in *The Later Work of Aubrey Beardsley*.
Oscar Wilde appears in the right-hand side of this drawing as Priapusa (Mrs. Marsuple in *The Savoy* instalments), Venus's inflated manicure and fardeuse.

CHAPTER II

OF THE MANNER IN WHICH VENUS WAS COIFFED AND PREPARED FOR SUPPER.

Before a toilet that shone like the altar of Nôtre Dame des Victoires, Venus was seated in a little dressing-gown of black and heliotrope. The coiffeur Cosmé was caring for her scented chevelure, and with tiny silver tongs, warm from the caresses of the flame, made delicious intelligent curls that fell as lightly as a breath about her forehead and over her eyebrows, and clustered like tendrils about her neck. Her three favourite girls, Pappelarde, Blanchemains, and Loreyne, waited immediately upon her with perfume and powder in delicate flaçons and frail cassolettes, and held in porcelain jars the ravishing paints prepared by Chateline for those cheeks and lips that had grown a little pale with anguish of exile. Her three favourite boys, Claude, Claire, and Sarrasine, stood amorously about with salver, fan and napkin. Millamant held a slight tray of slippers, Minette some tender gloves, La Popelinière, mistress of the robes, was ready with a frock of yellow and yellow. La Zambinella bore the jewels, Florizel some flowers, Amadour a box of various pins, and Vadius a box of sweets. Her doves, ever in attendance, walked about the room that was panelled with the gallant paintings of Jean Baptiste Dorat, and some dwarfs and doubtful creatures sat here and there, lolling out their tongues, pinching each other, and behaving oddly enough. Sometimes Venus gave them little smiles.

As the toilet was in progress, Priapusa, the fat manicure and fardeuse, strode in and seated herself by the side of the dressing-table, greeting Venus with an intimate nod. She wore a gown of white watered silk with gold lace trimmings, and a velvet necklet of false vermilion. Her hair hung in bandeaux over her ears, passing into a huge chignon at the back of her head, and the hat, wide-brimmed and hung with a vallance of pink muslin, was floral with red roses.

Priapusa's voice was full of salacious unction; she had terrible little gestures with the hands, strange movements with the shoulders, a short respiration that made surprising wrinkles in her bodice, a corrupt skin, large horny eyes, a parrot's nose, a small loose mouth, great flaccid cheeks, and chin after chin. She was a wise person, and Venus loved her more than any of her other servants, and had a hundred pet names for her, such as, Dear Toad, Pretty Pol, Cock-robin, Dearest Lip, Touchstone, Little Cough-drop, Bijou, Buttons, Dear Heart, Dick-dock, Mrs Manly, Little Nipper, Cochon-de-lait, Naughty-naughty, Blessèd Thing, and Trump.

The talk that passed between Priapusa and her mistress was of that excellent kind that passes between old friends, a perfect understanding giving to scraps of phrases their full meaning, and to the merest reference, a point. Naturally Tannhäuser, the new comer, was discussed a little. Venus had not seen him yet, and asked a score of questions on his account that were delightfully to the point.

Priapusa told the story of his sudden arrival, his curious wandering in the gardens, and calm satisfaction with all he saw there, his impromptu affection for a slender girl upon the first terrace, of the crowd of frocks that gathered round and pelted him with roses, of the graceful way he defended himself with his mask, and of the queer reverence he made to the statue of the God of all gardens, kissing that deity with a pilgrim's devotion. Just now Tannhäuser was at the baths, and was creating a most favourable impression.

The report and the coiffing were completed at the same moment.

"Cosmé," said Venus, "you have been quite sweet and quite brilliant, you have surpassed yourself to-night."

"Madam flatters me," replied the antique old thing, with a girlish giggle under his black satin mask. "Gad, Madam; sometimes I believe I have no talent in the world, but to-night I must confess to a touch of the vain mood."

It would pain me horribly to tell you about the painting of her face; suffice it that the sorrowful work was accomplished frankly, magnificently, and without a shadow of deception.

Venus slipped away the dressing-gown, and rose before the mirror in a flutter of frilled things. She was adorably tall and slender. Her neck and shoulders were so wonderfully drawn, and the little malicious breasts were full of the irritation of loveliness that can never be entirely comprehended, or ever enjoyed to the utmost. Her arms and hands were loosely but delicately articulated, and her legs were divinely long. From the hip to the knee, twenty-two inches; from the knee to the heel, twenty-two inches, as befitted a Goddess.

I should like to speak more particularly about her, for generalities are not of the slightest service in a description. But I am afraid that an enforced silence here and there would leave such numerous gaps in the picture that it had better not be begun at all than left unfinished.

Those who have only seen Venus in the Vatican, in the Louvre, in the Uffizi, or in the British Museum, can have no idea of how very beautiful and sweet she looked. Not at all like the lady in "Lemprière."

Priapusa grew quite lyric over the dear little person, and pecked at her arms with kisses.

"Dear Tongue, you must really behave yourself," said Venus and called Millamant to bring her the slippers.

The tray was freighted with the most exquisite and shapely pantoufles, sufficient to make Cluny a place of naught. There were shoes of grey and black and brown suède, of white silk and rose satin, and velvet and sarcenet; there were some of sea-green sewn with cherry blossoms, some of red with willow branches, and some of grey with bright-winged birds. There were heels of silver, of ivory, and of gilt; there were buckles of very precious stones set in most strange and esoteric devices; there were ribands tied and twisted into cunning forms; there were buttons so beautiful that the button-holes might have no pleasure till they closed upon them; there were soles of delicate leathers scented with maréchale, and linings of soft stuffs scented with the juice of July flowers. But Venus, finding none of them to her mind, called for a discarded pair of blood-red maroquin, diapered with pearls. These looked very distinguished over her white silk stockings.

As the tray was being carried away, the capricious Florizel snatched as usual a slipper from it, and fitted the foot over his penis, and made the necessary movements. That was Florizel's little caprice. Meantime, La Popelinière stepped forward with the frock.

"I shan't wear one to-night," said Venus. Then she slipped on her gloves.

When the toilet was at an end all her doves clustered round her feet, loving to frôler her ankles with their plumes, and the dwarfs clapped their hands, and put their fingers between their lips and whistled. Never before had Venus been so radiant and compelling. Spiridion, in the corner, looked up from his game of Spellicans and trembled.

Claude and Clair, pale with pleasure, stroked and touched her with their delicate hands, and wrinkled her stockings with their nervous lips, and smoothed them with their thin fingers; and Sarrasine undid her garters and kissed them inside and put them on again, pressing her thighs with his mouth. The dwarfs grew very daring, I can tell you. There was almost a mêlée. They illustrated pages 72 and 73 of Delvau's Dictionary.

In the middle of it all, Pranzmungel announced that supper was ready upon the fifth terrace. "Ah!" cried Venus, "I'm famished!"

The Fruit Bearers
original drawing (9¾ × 6⅞ in.) in the Scofield Thayer Collection, Fogg Art Museum, Harvard University, Cambridge, Massachusetts, U.S.A.
reproduced on p. 167 in *The Savoy*, no. 1 (January 1896), on p. 21 in *Under the Hill* (London, 1904) and as pl. 122 in *The Later Work of Aubrey Beardsley*.

CHAPTER III

HOW VENUS SUPPED; AND THEREAFTER WAS MIGHTILY AMUSED BY THE CURIOUS PRANKS OF HER ENTOURAGE.

She was quite delighted with Tannhäuser, and, of course, he sat next her at supper.

The terrace, made beautiful with a thousand vain and fantastical devices, and set with a hundred tables and four hundred couches, presented a truly splendid appearance. In the middle was a huge bronze fountain with three basins. From the first rose a many-breasted dragon, and four little Loves mounted upon swans, and each Love was furnished with a bow and arrow. Two of them that faced the monster seemed to recoil in fear, two that were behind made bold enough to aim their shafts at him. From the verge of the second sprang a circle of slim golden columns that supported silver doves, with tails and wings spread out. The third, held by a group of grotesquely attenuated satyrs, was centred with a thin pipe hung with masks and roses, and capped with children's heads.

From the mouths of the dragon and the Loves, from the swan's eyes, from the breasts of the doves, from the satyrs' horns and lips, from the masks at many points, and from the children's curls, the water played profusely, cutting strange arabesques and subtle figures.

The terrace was lit entirely by candles. There were four thousand of them, not numbering those upon the tables. The candlesticks were of a countless variety, and smiled with moulded cochônneries. Some were twenty feet high, and bore single candles that flared like fragrant torches over the feast, and guttered till the wax stood round the tops in tall lances. Some, hung with dainty petticoats of shining lustres, had a whole bevy of tapers upon them, devised in circles, in pyramids, in squares, in cuneiforms, in single lines regimentally and in crescents.

Then on quaint pedestals and Terminal Gods and gracious pilasters of every sort, were shell-like vases of excessive fruits and flowers that hung about and burst over the edges and could never be restrained. The orange-trees and myrtles, looped with vermilion sashes, stood in frail porcelain pots, and the rose-trees were wound and twisted with superb invention over trellis and standard. Upon one side of the terrace, a long gilded stage for the comedians was curtained off with Pagonian tapestries, and in front of it the music-stands were placed. The tables arranged between the fountain and the flight of steps to the sixth terrace were all circular, covered with white damask, and strewn with irises, roses, kingcups, colombines, daffodils, carnations and lilies; and the couches, high with soft cushions and spread with more stuffs than could be named, had fans thrown upon them, and little amorous surprise packets.

Beyond the escalier stretched the gardens, which were designed so elaborately and with so much splendour that the architect of the Fêtes d'Armailhacq could have found in them no matter for cavil, and the still lakes strewn with profuse barges full of gay flowers and wax marionettes, the alleys of tall trees, the arcades and cascades, the pavilions, the grottoes, and the garden-gods—all took a strange tinge of revelry from the glare of the light that fell upon them from the feast.

The frockless Venus and Tannhäuser, with Priapusa and Claude and Clair, and Farcy, the chief comedian, sat at the same table. Tannhäuser, who had doffed his travelling suit, wore long black silk stockings, a pair of pretty garters, a very elegant ruffled shirt, slippers and a wonderful dressing-gown. Claude and Clair wore nothing at all, delicious privilege of immaturity, and Farcy was in ordinary evening clothes. As for the rest of the company, it boasted some very noticeable dresses, and whole tables of quite delightful coiffures. There were spotted veils that seemed to stain the skin with some exquisite august disease, fans with eye-slits in them through which their bearers peeped and peered; fans painted with postures and covered with the sonnets of Sporion and the short stories of Scaramouche, and fans of big living moths stuck upon mounts of silver sticks. There were masks of green velvet that make the face look trebly powdered; masks of the heads of birds, of apes, of serpents, of dolphins, of men and women, of little embryons and of cats; masks like the faces of gods; masks of coloured glass, and masks of thin talc and of india-rubber. There were wigs of black and scarlet wools, of peacocks' feathers, of gold and silver threads, of swansdown, of the tendrils of the vine, and of human hairs; huge collars of stiff muslin rising high above the head; whole dresses of ostrich feathers curling inwards; tunics of panthers' skins that looked beautiful over pink tights; capotes of crimson satin trimmed with the wings of owls; sleeves cut into the shapes of apocryphal animals; drawers flounced down to the ankles, and flecked with tiny, red roses; stockings clocked with fêtes galantes, and curious designs, and petticoats cut like artificial flowers. Some of the women had put on delightful little moustaches dyed in purples and bright greens, twisted and waxed with absolute skill; and some wore great white beards after the manner of Saint Wilgeforte. Then Dorat had painted extraordinary grotesques and vignettes over their bodies, here and there. Upon a cheek, an old man scratching his horned head; upon a forehead, an old woman teased by an impudent amor; upon a shoulder, an amorous singerie; round a breast, a circlet of satyrs; about a wrist, a wreath of pale, unconscious babes; upon an elbow, a bouquet of spring flowers; across a back, some surprising scenes of adventure; at the corners of a mouth, tiny red spots; and upon a neck, a flight of birds, a caged parrot, a branch of fruit, a butterfly, a spider, a drunken dwarf, or, simply, some initials. But most wonderful of all were the black silhouettes painted upon the legs, and which showed through a white silk stocking like a sumptuous bruise.

The supper provided by the ingenious Rambouillet was quite beyond parallel. Never had he created a more exquisite menu. The *consommé impromptu* alone would have been sufficient to establish the immortal reputation of any chef. What, then, can I say of the *Dorade bouillie sauce maréchale*, the *ragoût aux langues de carpes*, the *ramereaux à la charnière*, the *ciboulette de gibier à l'espagnole*, the *paté de cuisses d'oie aux pois de Monsalvie*, the *queues d'agneau au clair de lune*, the *artichauts à la Grecque*, the *charlotte de pommes à la Lucy Waters*, the *bombes à la marée*, and the *glaces aux rayons d'or*? A veritable tour de cuisine that surpassed even the famous little suppers given by the Marquis de Réchale at Passy, and which the Abbé Mirliton pronounced "impeccable, and too good to be eaten."

Ah! Pierre Antoine Berquin de Rambouillet; you are worthy of your divine mistress!

Mere hunger quickly gave place to those finer instincts of the pure gourmet, and the strange wines cooled in buckets of snow unloosed all the décolleté spirits of astonishing conversation and atrocious laughter.

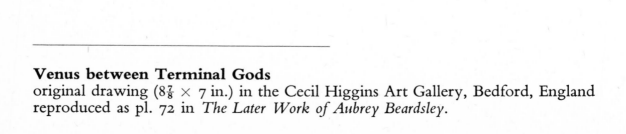

Venus between Terminal Gods
original drawing (8⅞ × 7 in.) in the Cecil Higgins Art Gallery, Bedford, England
reproduced as pl. 72 in *The Later Work of Aubrey Beardsley.*

VENUS.

CHAPTER IV

HOW THE COURT OF VENUS BEHAVED STRANGELY AT HER SUPPER.

At first there was the fun with the surprise packets that contained myriads of amusing things, then a general criticism of the decorations everyone finding a delightful meaning in the fall of festoon, turn of twig and twist of branch. Pulex, as usual, bore the palm for insight and invention, and to-night he was more brilliant than ever. He leant across the table and explained to the young page, Macfils de Martaga, what thing was intended by a certain arrangement of roses. The young page smiled and hummed the refrain of "La petite balette." Sporion, too, had delicate perceptions, and was vastly entertained by the disposition of the candelabra.

As the courses advanced, the conversation grew bustling and more personal. Pulex and Cyril and Marisca and Cathelin opened a fire of raillery. The infidelities of Cerise, the difficulties of Brancas, Sarmean's caprices that morning in the lily garden, Thorilliere's declining strength, Astarte's affection for Roseola, Felix's impossible member, Cathelin's passion for Sulpilia's poodle, Sola's passion for herself, the nasty bite that Marisca gave Chloe, the épilatiere of Pulex, Cyril's diseases, Butor's illness, Maryx's tiny cemetery, Lesbia's profound fourth letter, and a thousand amatory follies of the day were discussed.

From harsh and shrill and clamant, the voices grew blurred and inarticulate. Bad sentences were helped out by worse gestures, and at one table Scabius could only express himself with his napkin, after the manner of Sir Jolly Jumble in the "Soldier's Fortune" of Otway. Basalissa and Lysistrata tried to pronounce each other's names, and became very affectionate in the attempt, and Tala, the tragedian, robed in ample purple, and wearing plume and buskin, rose to his feet, and with swaying gestures began to recite one of his favourite parts. He got no further than the first line, but repeated it again and again, with fresh accents and intonations each time, and was only silenced by the approach of the asparagus that was being served by satyrs costumed in white muslin.

Clitor and Sodon had a violent struggle over the beautiful Pella, and nearly upset a chandelier. Sophie became very intimate with an empty champagne bottle, swore it had made her enciente, and ended by having a mock accouchment on the top of the table; and Belamour pretended to be a dog, and pranced from couch to couch on all fours, biting and barking and licking. Mellefont crept about dropping love philtres into glasses. Juventus and Ruella stripped and put on each other's things, Spelto offered a prize for whoever should come first, and Spelto won it! Tannhäuser, just a little grisé, lay down on the cushions and let Julia do whatever she liked.

I wish I could be allowed to tell you what occurred round table 15, just at this moment. It would amuse you very much, and would give you a capital idea of the habits of Venus' retinue. Indeed, for deplorable reasons, by far the greater part of what was said and done at this supper must remain unrecorded and even unsuggested.

Venus allowed most of the dishes to pass untasted, she was so engaged with the beauty of Tannhäuser. She laid her head many times on his robe, kissing him passionately; and his skin at once firm and yielding, seemed to those exquisite little teeth of hers, the most incomparable pasture. Her upper lip curled and trembled with excitement, showing the gums. Tannhäuser, on his side, was no less devoted. He adored her all over and all the things she had on, and buried his face in the folds and flounces of her linen, and ravished away a score of frills in his excess. He found her exasperating, and crushed her in his arms, and slaked his parched lips at her mouth. He caressed her eyelids softly with his finger tips, and pushed aside the curls from her forehead, and did a thousand gracious things, tuning her body as a violinist tunes his instrument before he plays upon it.

Priapusa snorted like an old war horse at the sniff of powder, and tickled Tannhäuser and Venus by turns, and slipped her tongue down their throats, and refused to be quiet at all until she had had a mouthful of the Chevalier. Claude, seizing his chance, dived under the table and came up the other side just under the queen's couch, and before she could say "One!" he was taking his coffee "aux deux colonnes." Clair was furious at his friend's success, and sulked for the rest of the evening.

CHAPTER V

OF THE BALLET
DANCED BY THE
SERVANTS OF VENUS.

After the fruits and fresh wines had been brought in by a troop of woodland creatures, decked with green leaves and all sorts of Spring flowers, the candles in the orchestra were lit, and in another' moment the musicians bustled into their places. The wonderful Titurel de Schentefleur was the chef d'orchestre, and the most insidious of conductors. His bâton dived into a phrase and brought out the most magical and magnificent things, and seemed rather to play every instrument than to lead it. He could add a grace even to Scarlatti and a wonder to Beethoven. A delicate, thin, little man with thick lips and a nez retroussé, with long black hair and curled moustache, in the manner of Molière. What were his amatory tastes, no one in the Venusberg could tell. He generally passed for a virgin, and Cathos had nicknamed him "The Solitaire."

To-night he appeared in a court suit of white silk, brilliant with decorations. His hair was curled into resplendent ringlets that trembled like springs at the merest gesture of his arm, and in his ears swung the diamonds given him by Venus.

The orchestra was, as usual, in its uniform of red vest and breeches trimmed with gold lace, white stockings and red shoes. Titurel had written a ballet for the evening's divertissement, founded upon De Bergerac's comedy of "Les Bacchanales de Fanfreluche," in which the action and dances were designed by him as well as the music.

I

The curtain rose upon a scene of rare beauty, a remote Arcadian valley, and watered with a dear river as fresh and pastoral as a perfect fifth of this scrap of Tempe. It was early morning, and the re-arisen sun, like the prince in the "Sleeping Beauty," woke all the earth with his lips. In that golden embrace the night dews were caught up and made splendid, the trees were awakened from their obscure dreams, the

43

slumber of the birds was broken, and all the flowers of the valley rejoiced, forgetting their fear of the darkness.

Suddenly, to the music of pipe and horn, a troop of satyrs stepped out from the recesses of the woods, bearing in their hands nuts and green boughs and flowers and roots and whatsoever the forest yielded, to heap upon the altar of the mysterious Pan that stood in the middle of the stage; and from the hills came down the shepherds and shepherd-esses, leading their flocks and carrying garlands upon their crooks. Then a rustic priest, white-robed and venerable, came slowly across the valley followed by a choir of radiant children.

The scene was admirably stage-managed, and nothing could have been more varied yet harmonious than this Arcadian group. The service was quaint and simple, but with sufficient ritual to give the corps-de-ballet an opportunity of showing its dainty skill. The dancing of the satyrs was received with huge favour, and when the priest raised his hand in final blessing, the whole troop of worshippers made such an intricate and elegant exit that it was generally agreed that Titurel had never before shown so fine an invention.

Scarcely had the stage been empty for a moment, when Sporion entered, followed by a brilliant rout of dandies and smart women. Sporion was a tall, slim, depraved young man with a slight stoop, a troubled walk, an oval impassable face, with its olive skin drawn tightly over the bone, strong scarlet lips, long Japanese eyes, and a great gilt toupet. Round his shoulders hung a high-collared satin cape of salmon pink, with long black ribands untied and floating about his body. His coat of sea-green spotted muslin was caught in at the waist by a scarlet sash with scalloped edges, and frilled out over the hips for about six inches. His trousers, loose and wrinkled, reached to the end of the calf, and were brocaded down the sides, and ruched magnificently

Design for a front cover of *The Yellow Book* (unused)
original drawing (7⅝ × 6⅛ in.) in the Princeton University Library, Princeton, New Jersey, U.S.A.
reproduced as pl. 76 in *The Early Work of Aubrey Beardsley*.
Although designed by Beardsley as a front cover for *The Yellow Book*, this drawing was never used. It contains the whimsical conceit of including (prematurely) a copy of the at most barely begun *Story of Venus and Tannhäuser* along with volumes of Shakespeare and Dickens. The other tomes are *The Yellow Book* itself and *Discords*, a novel published in 1894 and written by Mary Chavelita Bright under the pseudonym "George Egerton."

at the ankles. The stockings were of white kid, with stalls for the toes, and had delicate red sandles strapped over them. But his little hands, peeping out from their frills, seemed quite the most insinuating things, such supple fingers tapering to the point, with tiny nails stained pink, such unquenchable palms, lined and mounted like Lord Fanny's in "Love at all Hazards," and such blue-veined, hairless backs! In his left hand he carried a small lace handkerchief broidered with a coronet.

As for his friends and followers they made the most superb and insolent crowd imaginable, but to catalogue the clothes they had on would require a chapter as long as the famous tenth in Pénillière's history of underlinen. On the whole they looked a very distinguished chorus.

Sporion stepped forward and explained with swift and various gesture that he and his friends were tired of the amusements, wearied with the poor pleasures offered by the civil world, and had invaded the Arcadian valley hoping to experience a new frisson in the destruction of some shepherd's or some satyr's naiveté, and the infusion of their venom among the dwellers of the woods.

The chorus assented with languid but expressive movements.

Curious, and not a little frightened, at the arrival of the worldly company, the sylvans began to peep nervously through the branches of the trees, and one or two fauns and a shepherd or so crept out warily. Sporion and all the ladies and gentlemen made enticing sounds and invited the rustic creatures with all the grace in the world to come and join them. By little batches they came, lured by the strange looks, by the scents and the doings, and by the brilliant clothes, and some ventured quite near, timorously fingering the delicious textures of the stuffs. Then Sporion and each of his friends took a satyr or a shepherd or something by the hand, and made the preliminary steps of a courtly measure, for which the most admirable combinations had been invented, and the most charming music written.

The pastoral folk were entirely bewildered when they saw such restrained and graceful movements, and made the most grotesque and futile efforts to imitate them.

Dio mio, a pretty sight! A charming effect too was obtained by the intermixture of stockinged calf and hairy leg, of rich brocade bodice and plain blouse, of tortured head-dress and loose untutored locks.

When the dance was ended, the servants of Sporion brought on champagne, and, with many pirouettes, poured it magnificently into slender glasses, and tripped about plying those Arcadian mouths that had never before tasted such a royal drink.

* * * * *

Then the curtain fell with a pudic rapidity.

II

'Twas not long before the invaders began to enjoy the first fruits of their expedition, plucking them in the most seductive manner with their smooth fingers, and feasting lip and tongue and tooth, whilst the shepherds and satyrs and shepherdesses fairly gasped under the new joys, for the pleasure they experienced was almost too keen and too profound for their simple and untilled natures. Fanfreluche and the rest of the rips and ladies tingled with excitement and frolicked like young lambs in a fresh meadow. Again and again the wine was danced round, and the valley grew as busy as a market day. Attracted by the noise and merrymaking, all those sweet infants I told you of, skipped suddenly on to the stage, and began clapping their hands and laughing immoderately at the passion and the disorder and commotion, and mimicking the nervous staccato movements they saw in their pretty childish way.

In a flash, Fanfreluche disentangled himself and sprang to his feet, gesticulating as if he would say, "Ah, the little dears!" "Ah, the rorty little things!" "Ah, the little ducks!" for he was so fond of children. Scarcely had he caught one by the thigh than a quick rush was made by everybody for the succulent limbs; and how they tousled them and mousled them! The children cried out, I can tell you. Of course there were not enough for everybody, so some had to share, and some had simply to go on with what they were doing before.

I must not, by the way, forget to mention the independent attitude

---

A Footnote
reproduced on p. 185 (immediately preceding the instalment of "Under the Hill") in *The Savoy*, no. 2 (April 1896) and as pl. 126 in *The Later Work of Aubrey Beardsley*.

taken by six or seven of the party, who sat and stood about with half-closed eyes, inflated nostrils, clenched teeth, and painful, parted lips, behaving like the Duc de Broglio when he watched the amours of the Regent d'Orleans.

Now as Fanfreluche and his friends began to grow tired and exhausted with the new debauch, they cared no longer to take the initiative, but, relaxing every muscle, abandoned themselves to passive joys, yielding utterly to the ardent embraces of the intoxicated satyrs, who waxed fast and furious, and seemed as if they would never come to the end of their strength. Full of the new tricks they had learnt that morning, they played them passionately and roughly, making havoc of the cultured flesh, and tearing the splendid frocks and dresses into ribands. Duchesses and Maréchales, Marquises and Princesses, Dukes and Marshals, Marquesses and Princes, were ravished and stretched and rumpled and crushed beneath the interminable vigour and hairy breasts of the inflamed woodlanders. They bit at the white thighs and nozzled wildly in the crevices. They sat astride the women's chests and consummated frantically with their bosoms; they caught their prey by the hips and held it over their heads, irrumating with prodigious gusto. It was the triumph of the valley.

High up in the heavens the sun had mounted and filled all the air with generous warmth, whilst shadows grew shorter and sharper. Little light-winged papillons flitted across the stage, the bees made music on their flowery way, the birds were very gay and kept up a jargoning and refraining, the lambs were bleating upon the hill side, and the orchestra kept playing, playing the uncanny tunes of Titurel.

CHAPTER VI

OF THE AMOROUS ENCOUNTER WHICH
TOOK PLACE BETWEEN VENUS AND TANNHÄUSER.

Venus and Tannhäuser had retired to the exquisite little boudoir or pavilion Le Con had designed for the queen on the first terrace, and which commanded the most delicious view of the parks and gardens. It was a sweet little place, all silk curtains and soft cushions. There were eight sides to it, bright with mirrors and candelabra, and rich with pictured panels, and the ceiling, dome shaped and some thirty feet above the head, shone obscurely with gilt mouldings through the warm haze of candle light below. Tiny wax statuettes dressed theatrically and smiling with plump cheeks, quaint magots that looked as cruel as foreign gods, gilded monticules, pale celadon vases, clocks that said nothing, ivory boxes full of secrets, china figures playing whole scenes of plays, and a world of strange preciousness crowded the curious cabinets that stood against the walls. On one side of the room there were six perfect little card tables, with quite the daintiest and most elegant chairs set primly round them; so, after all, there may be some truth in that line of Mr. Theodore Watts,—

"I played at picquet with the Queen of Love"

Nothing in the pavilion was more beautiful than the folding screens painted by De La Pine, with Claudian landscapes—the sort of things that fairly make one melt, things one can lie and look at for hours together, and forget the country can ever be dull and tiresome. There were four of them, delicate walls that hem in an amour so cosily, and make room within room.

The place was scented with huge branches of red roses, and with a faint amatory perfume breathed out from the couches and cushions—a perfume Chateline distilled in secret and called L'Eau Lavante.

Return of Tannhäuser to the Venusberg (first version)
original wash drawing in the Rosenwald Collection, National Gallery of Art, Washington D.C., U.S.A.
reproduced as pl. 70 in *The Later Work of Aubrey Beardsley*.
This drawing, dated 1891, comes from Beardsley's period as an amateur artist, although its composition served as a basis for the second and better-known version.

Those who have only seen Venus at the Louvre or the British Museum, at Florence, at Naples, or at Rome, can have not the faintest idea how sweet and enticing and gracious, how really exquisitely beautiful she looked lying with Tannhäuser upon rose silk in that pretty boudoir.

Cosmé's precise curls and artful waves had been finally disarranged at supper, and strayed ringlets of the black hair fell loosely over her soft, delicious, tired, swollen eyelids. Her frail chemise and dear little drawers were torn and moist, and clung transparently about her, and all her body was nervous and responsive. Her closed thighs seemed like a vast replica of the little bijou she held between them; the beautiful tétons du derrière were as firm as a plump virgin's cheek, and promised a joy as profound as the mystery of the Rue Vendôme, and the minor chevelure, just profuse enough, curled as prettily as the hair upon a cherub's head.

Tannhäuser, pale and speechless with excitement, passed his gem-girt fingers brutally over the divine limbs, tearing away smock and pantaloon and stocking, and then, stripping himself of his own few things, fell upon the splendid lady with a deep-drawn breath!

It is, I know, the custom of all romancers to paint heroes who can give a lady proof of their valliance at least twenty times a night. Now Tannhäuser had no such Gargantuan facility, and was rather relieved when, an hour later, Priapusa and Doricourt and some others burst drunkenly into the room and claimed Venus for themselves. The pavilion soon filled with a noisy crowd that could scarcely keep its feet. Several of the actors were there, and Lesfesses, who had played Fan-freluche so brilliantly, and was still in his makeup, paid tremendous attention to Tannhäuser. But the Chevalier found him quite uninteresting off the stage, and rose and crossed the room to where Venus and the manicure were seated.

"How tired the dear baby looks," said Priapusa. "Shall I put him in his little cot?"

"Well, if he's as sleepy as I am," yawned Venus, "you can't do better."

Priapusa lifted her mistress off the pillows, and carried her in her arms in a nice, motherly way.

"Come along, children," said the fat old thing, "come along; it's time you were both in bed."

CHAPTER VII

HOW TANNHÄUSER AWAKENED
AND TOOK HIS MORNING ABLUTIONS
IN THE VENUSBERG.

It is always delightful to wake up in a new bedroom. The fresh wall paper, the strange pictures, the positions of doors and windows—imperfectly grasped the night before—are revealed with all the charm of surprise when we open our eyes the next morning.

It was about eleven o'clock when Tannhäuser awoke and stretched himself deliciously in his great plumed four-post bed, and nursed his waking thoughts, that stared at the curious patterned canopy above him. He was very pleased with the room, which certainly was chic and fascinating, and recalled the voluptuous interiors of the elegant amorous Baudouin. Through the tiny parting of the long, flowered window curtains, the Chevalier caught a peep of the sun-lit lawns outside, the silver fountains, the bright flowers, and the gardeners at work.

"Quiet sweet," he murmured, and turned round to freshen the frilled silk pillows behind him.

He thought of the "Romaunt de la Rose," beautiful, but all too brief.

Of the Claude in Lady Delaware's collection.[1]

Of a wonderful pair of blonde trousers he would get Madame Belleville to make for him.

Of a mysterious park full of faint echoes and romantic sounds.

Of a great stagnant lake that must have held the subtlest frogs that ever were, and was surrounded with dark unreflected trees, and sleeping fleurs de luce.

Of Saint Rose, the well-known Peruvian virgin; how she vowed

---

[1] *The chef d'œuvre, it seems to me, of an adorable and impeccable master, who more than any other landscape-painter puts us out of conceit with our cities, and makes us forget the country can be graceless and dull and tiresome. That he should ever have been compared unfavourably with Turner—the Wiertz of landscape-painting—seems almost incredible. Corot is Claude's only worthy rival, but he does not eclipse or supplant the earlier master. A painting of Corot's is like an exquisite lyric poem, full of love and truth; whilst one of Claude's recalls some noble eclogue glowing with rich concentrated thought.*

herself to perpetual virginity when she was four years old[2]; how she was beloved by Mary, who from the pale fresco in the Church of Saint Dominic, would stretch out her arms to embrace her; how she built a little oratory at the end of the garden and prayed and sang hymns in it till all the beetles, spiders, snails and creeping things came round to listen; how she promised to marry Ferdinand de Flores, and on the bridal morning perfumed herself and painted her lips, and put on her wedding frock, and decked her hair with roses, and went up to a little hill not far without the walls of Lima; how she knelt there some moments calling tenderly upon Our Lady's name, and how Saint Mary descended and kissed Rose upon the forehead and carried her up swiftly into heaven.

He thought of the splendid opening of Racine's "Britannicus."

Of a strange pamphlet he had found in Venus's library, called "A Plea for the Domestication of the Unicorn."

Of the "Bacchanals of Sporion."[3]

Of Morales' Madonnas with their high egg-shaped creamy foreheads and well-crimped silken hair.

Of Rossini's "Stabat Mater" (that delightful *demodé* piece of decadence, with a quality in its music like the bloom upon wax fruit).

Of love, and of a hundred other things.

Then his half-closed eyes wandered among the prints that hung upon the rose-striped walls. Within the delicate, curved frames lived the corrupt and gracious creatures of Dorat and his school; slim children in masque and domino, smiling horribly, exquisite lechers leaning over

---

2 *"At an age," writes Dubonnet, "when girls are for the most part well confirmed in all the hateful practices of coquetry, and attend with gusto, rather than with distaste, the hideous desires and terrible satisfactions of men!"*

All who would respire the perfumes of Saint Rose's sanctity, and enjoy the story of the adorable intimacy that subsisted between her and Our Lady, should read Mother Ursula's "Ineffable and Miraculous Life of the Flower of Lima," published shortly after the canonisation of Rose by Pope Clement X, in 1671. "Truly," exclaims the famous nun, "to chronicle the girlhood of this holy virgin makes as delicate a task as to trace the forms of some slim, sensitive plant, whose lightness, sweetness and simplicity defy and trouble the most cunning pencil." Mother Ursula certainly acquits herself of the task with wonderful delicacy and taste. A cheap reprint of the biography has lately been brought out by Chaillot and Son.

3 *A comedy ballet in one act by Philippe Savaral and Titurel de Schentefleur. The Marquis de Vandésir, who was present at the first performance, has left us a short impression of it in his* Mémoires.

the shoulders of smooth doll-like ladies, and doing nothing particular, terrible little pierrots posing as mulierasts, or pointing at something outside the picture, and unearthly fops and strange women mingling in some rococo room lighted mysteriously by the flicker of a dying fire that throws huge shadows upon wall and ceiling. One of the prints showing how an old marquis practised the five-finger exercise, while in front of him his mistress offered her warm fesses to a panting poodle, made the chevalier stroke himself a little.

Tannhäuser had taken some books to bed with him. One was the witty, extravagant, "Tuesday and Josephine," another was the score of "The Rheingold." Making a pulpit of his knees he propped up the opera before him and turned over the pages with a loving hand, and found it delicious to attack Wagner's brilliant comedy with the cool head of the morning.[4] Once more he was ravished with the beauty and wit of the opening scene; the mystery of its prelude that seems to come up from the very mud of the Rhine, and to be as ancient, the abominable primitive wantonness of the music that follows the talk and movements of the Rhine-maidens, the black, hateful sounds of Alberich's love-making, and the flowing melody of the river of legends.

But it was the third tableau that he applauded most that morning, the scene where Loge, like some flamboyant primeval Scapin, practises his cunning upon Alberich. The feverish insistent ringing of the hammers at the forge, the dry staccato restlessness of Mime, the ceaseless coming and going of the troup of Niblungs, drawn hither and thither like a flock of terror-stricken and infernal sheep. Alberich's savage activity and metamorphoses, and Loge's rapid, flaming tongue-like movements, make the tableau the least reposeful, most troubled and confusing thing in the whole range of opera. How the Chevalier rejoiced in the extravagant monstrous poetry, the heated melodrama, and splendid agitation of it all!

After the chevalier got up, he slipped off his dainty night-dress, posturing elegantly before a long mirror, and made much of himself. Now he would bend forward, now lie upon the floor, now stand up-

---

[4] *It is a thousand pities that concerts should only be given either in the afternoon, when you are torpid, or in the evening, when you are nervous. Surely you should assist at fine music as you assist at the Mass—before noon—when your brain and heart are not too troubled and tired with the secular influences of the growing day.*

right, and now rest upon one leg and let the other hang loosely till he looked as if he might have been drawn by some early Italian master. Anon he would lie upon the floor with his back to the glass, and glance amorously over his shoulder. Then with a white silk sash he draped himself in a hundred charming ways. So engrossed was he with his mirrored shape that he had not noticed the entrance of a troop of serving boys, who stood admiringly but respectfully at a distance, ready to receive his waking orders. As soon as the chevalier observed them he smiled sweetly, and bade them prepare his bath.

The bathroom was the largest and perhaps the most beautiful apartment in his splendid suite. The well-known engraving by Lorette that forms the frontispiece to Millevoye's "Architecture du XVIIIme siècle," will give you a better idea than any words of mine of the construction and decoration of the room. Only, in Lorette's engraving, the bath sunk into the middle of the floor is a little too small.

Tannhäuser stood for a moment, like Narcissus, gazing at his reflection in the still scented water, and then just ruffling its smooth surface with one foot, stepped elegantly into the cool basin, and swam round it twice, very gracefully.

"Won't you join me?" he said, turning to those beautiful boys who stood ready with warm towels and perfume. In a moment they were free of their light morning dress, and jumped into the water and joined hands, and surrounded the Chevalier with a laughing chain.

"Splash me a little," he cried, and the boys teased him with water and quite excited him. He chased the prettiest of them and bit his fesses, and kissed him upon the perineum till the dear fellow banded like a carmelite, and its little bald top-knot looked like a great pink pearl under the water. As the boy seemed anxious to take up the active attitude, Tannhäuser graciously descended to the passive—a generous trait that won him the complete affections of his valets de bain, or pretty fish, as he called them, because they loved to swim between his legs.

However, it is not so much at the very bath itself, as in the drying and delicious frictions, that the bather finds his chiefest pleasures, and Tannhäuser was more than satisfied with the skill his attendants displayed in the performance of those quasi amorous functions. The delicate attention they paid his loving parts aroused feelings within him that almost amounted to gratitude; and when the rites were ended any touch of home-sickness he might have felt before was utterly dispelled.

After he had rested a little, and sipped his chocolate, he wandered into the dressing-room. Daucourt, his valet de chambre, Chenille, the perruquier and barber, and two charming young dressers, were awaiting him and ready with suggestions for the morning toilet. The shaving over, Daucourt commanded his underlings to step forward with the suite of suits from which he proposed Tannhäuser should make a choice. The final selection was a happy one. A dear little coat of pigeon rose silk that hung loosely about his hips, and showed off the jut of his behind to perfection; trousers of black lace in flounces, falling—almost like a petticoat—as far as the knee; and a delicate chemise of white muslin, spangled with gold and profusely pleated.

The two dressers, under Daucourt's direction, did their work superbly, beautifully, leisurely, with an exquisite deference for the nude, and a really sensitive appreciation of Tannhäuser's scrumptious torso.

The Ascension of Saint Rose of Lima
reproduced on p. 189 in *The Savoy*, no. 2 (April 1896), on p. 27 in *Under the Hill* (London, 1904) and as pl. 124 in *The Later Work of Aubrey Beardsley*.
Beardsley's account of St. Rose of Lima differs considerably from the accepted version. Christened Isabella de Santa Maria de Flores, St. Rose (1586–1617) was the first American-born saint. Although she refused to marry, as Beardsley pointed out, in actuality instead of ascending to heaven with the Virgin, she joined the Dominicans as a tertiary and moved into a shack in her garden, where she practised extreme mortification and penance. These rigours undermined her health, but also brought her a reputation for saintliness and for the possession of supernatural and mystical powers. She was canonised by Clement X in 1671.

CHAPTER VIII

OF THE ECSTASY OF ADOLPHE, AND THE RE-MARKABLE MANIFESTATION THEREOF.

When all was said and done, the Chevalier tripped off to bid good morning to Venus. He found her wandering, in a sweet white muslin frock, upon the lawn outside, plucking flowers to deck her little déjeuner. He kissed her lightly upon the neck.

"I'm just going to feed Adolphe," she said, pointing to a little reticule of buns that hung from her arm. Adolphe was her pet unicorn. "He is such a dear," she continued; "milk-white all over excepting his black eyes, rose mouth and nostrils, and scarlet John."

The unicorn had a very pretty palace of its own, made of green foliage and golden bars—a fitting home for such a delicate and dainty beast. Ah, it was indeed a splendid thing to watch the white creature roaming in its artful cage, proud and beautiful, and knowing no mate except the Queen herself.

As Venus and Tannhäuser approached the wicket, Adolphe began prancing and curvetting, pawing the soft turf with his ivory hoofs, and flaunting his tail like a gonfalon. Venus raised the latch and entered.

"You mustn't come in with me—Adolphe is so jealous," she said, turning to the Chevalier who was following her; "but you can stand outside and look on; Adolphe likes an audience." Then in her delicious fingers she broke the spicy buns, and with affectionate niceness, break-fasted her ardent pet. When the last crumbs had been scattered, Venus brushed her hands together and pretended to leave the cage, without taking any more notice of Adolphe. Every morning she went through this piece of play, and every morning the amorous unicorn was cheated into a distressing agony lest that day should have proved the last of Venus's love. Not for long, though, would she leave him in that doubt-ful, piteous state, but running back passionately to where he stood, make adorable amends for her unkindness.

Poor Adolphe! How happy he was, touching the Queen's breasts with his quick tongue-tip. I have no doubt that the keener scent of animals must make women much more attractive to them than to men; for the gorgeous odour that but faintly fills our nostrils must be revealed to the brute creation in divine fulness. Anyhow, Adolphe sniffed as never a man did around the skirts of Venus. After the first charming interchange of affectionate delicacies was over, the unicorn lay down upon his side, and, closing his eyes, beat his stomach wildly with the mark of manhood!

Venus caught that stunning member in her hands and lay her cheek along it; but few touches were wanted to consummate the creature's pleasure. The Queen bared her left arm to the elbow, and with the soft underneath of it made amazing movements horizontally upon the tightly-strung instrument. When the melody began to flow, the unicorn offered up an astonishing vocal accompaniment. Tannhäuser was amused to learn that the etiquette of the Venusberg compelled everybody to await the outburst of these venereal sounds before they could sit down to déjeuner.

Adolphe had been quite profuse that morning.

Venus knelt where it had fallen, and lapped her little aperitif!

The Third Tableau of "Das Rheingold"
original drawing (10 × 6⅞ in.) in the Museum of Art, Rhode Island School of Design, Providence, Rhode Island, U.S.A.
reproduced on p. 193 in *The Savoy*, no. 2 (April 1896), on p. 33 in *Under the Hill* (London, 1904) and as pl. 125 in *The Later Work of Aubrey Beardsley*.
This drawing illustrates an important scene from "Das Rheingold," the prelude to Wagner's "Der Ring des Nibelungen." Wotan and Loge have descended to the Nibelheim to steal the horde of gold which the dwarf Alberich had seized from the Rheinmädchen. Alberich has fashioned part of the Rheingold into the ring, which gives mastery over the world, and into the tarnhelm, which enables the wearer to appear in any form he chooses. Wotan and Loge trick Alberich into using the tarnhelm, and the dwarf transforms himself first into a huge serpent (illustrated here) and then into a frog, in which form he is captured by Wotan and Loge, who take his treasure and use it to pay the giants, Fasolt and Fafner, for the building of Valhalla.

CHAPTER IX

HOW VENUS AND TANNHÄUSER BREAKFASTED AND THEN DROVE THROUGH THE PALACE GARDENS.

The breakfasters were scattered over the gardens in têtes-a-têtes and tiny parties. Venus and Tannhäuser sat together upon the lawn that lay in front of the Casino, and made havoc of a ravishing déjeuner. The Chevalier was feeling very happy. Everything around him seemed so white and light and matinal; the floating frocks of the ladies, the scarce robed boys and satyrs stepping hither and thither elegantly, with meats and wines and fruits; the damask tablecloths, the delicate talk and laughter that rose everywhere; the flowers' colour and the flowers' scent; the shady trees, the wind's cool voice, and the sky above that was as fresh and pastoral as a perfect fifth. And Venus looked so beautiful. Not at all like the lady in Lemprière.

"You're such a dear!" murmured Tannhäuser, holding her hand.

At the further end of the lawn, a little hidden by a rose-tree, a young man was breakfasting alone. He toyed nervously with his food now and then, but for the most part leant back in his chair with unemployed hands, and gazed stupidly at Venus.

"That's Felix," said the Goddess in answer to an enquiry from the Chevalier; and she went on to explain his attitude. Felix always attended Venus upon her little latrinal excursions, holding her, serving her, and making much of all she did. To undo her things, lift her skirts, to wait and watch the coming, to dip a lip or finger in the royal output, to stain himself deliciously with it, to lie beneath her as the favours fell, to carry off the crumped, crotted paper; these were the pleasures of that young man's life.

Truly there never was a queen so beloved by her subjects as Venus. Everything she wore had its lover. Heavens! how her handkerchiefs were filched, her stockings stolen! Daily, what intrigues, what countless ruses to possess her merest frippery! Every scrap of her body was adored. Never, for Savaral, could her ear yield sufficient wax! Never, for Pradon, could she spit prodigally enough! And Saphius found a month an interminable time.

After breakfast was over, and Felix's fears lest Tannhäuser should have robbed him of his capricious rights had been dispelled, Venus invited the Chevalier to take a more extensive view of the gardens, parks, pavilions, and ornamental waters. The carriage was ordered. It was a delicate, shell-like affair, with billowy cushions and a light canopy, and was drawn by ten satyrs, dressed as finely as the coachmen of the Empress Pauline the First.

The drive proved interesting and various, and Tannhäuser was quite delighted with almost everything he saw.

And who is not pleased when on either side of him rich lawns are spread with lovely frocks and white limbs, and upon flower-beds the dearest ladies are implicated in a glory of underclothing,—when he can see in the deep cool shadow of the trees warm boys entwined, here at the base, there in the branch,—when in the fountain's wave Love, holds his court, and the insistent water burrows in every delicious crease and crevice?

A pretty sight, too, was little Rosalie perched like a postilion upon the painted phallus of the god of all gardens. Her eyes were closed and she was smiling as the carriage passed. Round her neck and slender girlish shoulders there was a cloud of complex dress, over which bulged her wig-like flaxen tresses. Her legs and feet were bare, and the toes twisted in an amorous style. At the foot of the statue lay her shoes and stockings and a few other things.

Tannhäuser was singularly moved at this spectacle, and rose out of all proportion. Venus slipped the fingers of comfort under the lace flounces of his trousers, saying, "It it all mine? Is it all mine?" and doing fascinating things. In the end, the carriage was only prevented from being overturned by the happy intervention of Priapusa who stepped out from somewhere or other just in time to preserve its balance.

How the old lady's eye glistened as Tannhäuser withdrew his panting blade! In her sincere admiration for fine things, she forgot and forgave the shock she had received from the falling of the gay equipage. Venus

---

Venus
original drawing (4⅜ × 3⅛ in.) in the Grenville L. Winthrop Bequest, Fogg Art Museum, Harvard University, Cambridge, Massachusetts, U.S.A.
reproduced on p. 260 in *The Studio*, vol. XIII (1898) and as pl. 93 in *The Early Work of Aubrey Beardsley.*

and Tannhäuser were profuse with apology and thanks, and quite a crowd of loving courtiers gathered round, consoling and congratulating in a breath.

The Chevalier vowed he never would go in the carriage again, and was really quite upset about it. However, after he had had a little support from the smelling-salts, he recovered his self-possession, and consented to drive on further.

The landscape grew rather mysterious. The park, no longer troubled and adorned with figures, was full of grey echoes and mysterious sounds, the leaves whispered a little sadly, and there was a grotto that murmured like the voice that haunts the silence of a deserted oracle. Tannhäuser became a little triste. In the distance, through the trees, gleamed a still, argent lake—a reticent, romantic water that must have held the subtlest fish that ever were. Around its marge the trees and flags and fleurs de luce were unbreakably asleep.

The Chevalier fell into a strange mood, as he looked at the lake. It seemed to him that the thing would speak, reveal some curious secret, say some beautiful word, if he should dare wrinkle its pale face with a pebble.

"I should be frightened to do that, though," he said to himself. Then he wondered what there might be upon the other side; other gardens, other gods? A thousand drowsy fancies passed through his brain. Sometimes the lake took fantastic shapes, or grew to twenty times its size, or shrunk into a miniature of itself, without ever once losing its unruffled calm, its deathly reserve. When the water increased, the Chevalier was very frightened, for he thought how huge the frogs must have become. He thought of their big eyes and monstrous wet feet, but when the water lessened, he laughed to himself, whilst thinking how tiny the frogs must have grown. He thought of their legs that must look thinner than spiders', and of their dwindled croaking that never could be heard. Perhaps the lake was only painted, after all. He had seen things like it at the theatre. Anyhow, it was a wonderful lake, a beautiful lake, and he would love to bathe in it, but he was sure he would be drowned if he did.

CHAPTER X

OF THE "STABAT MATER", SPIRIDION, AND DE LA PINE.

When he awoke up from his day-dreams, he noticed that the carriage was on its way back to the palace. They stopped at the Casino first, and stepped out to join the players at petits chevaux. Tannhäuser preferred to watch the game rather than play himself, and stood behind Venus, who slipped into a vacant chair and cast gold pieces upon lucky numbers. The first thing that Tannhäuser noticed was the grace and charm, the gaiety and beauty of the croupiers. They were quite adorable even when they raked in one's little losings. Dressed in black silk, and wearing white kid gloves, loose yellow wigs and feathered toques: with faces oval and young, bodies lithe and quick, voices silvery and affectionate, they made amends for all the hateful arrogance, disgusting aplomb, and shameful ugliness of the rest of their kind.

The dear fellow who proclaimed the winner was really quite delightful. He took a passionate interest in the horses, and had licked all the paint off their petits couillons!

You will ask me, no doubt, "Is that all he did?" I will answer, "Not quite," as the merest glance at their petits derrières would prove.

In the afternoon light that came through the great silken-blinded windows of the Casino, all the gilded decorations, all the chandeliers, the mirrors, the polished floor, the painted ceiling, the horses galloping round their green meadow, the fat rouleaux of gold and silver, the ivory rakes, the fanned and strange-frocked crowd of dandy gamesters looked magnificently rich and warm. Tea was being served. It was so pretty to see some plushed little lady sipping nervously, and keeping her eyes over the cup's edge intently upon the slackening horses. The more indifferent left the tables and took their tea in parties here and there.

Tannhäuser found a great deal to amuse him at the Casino. Ponchon was the manager, and a person of extraordinary invention. Never a day

Return of Tannhäuser to the Venusberg (second version)
original wash drawing ($5\frac{1}{4} \times 5\frac{3}{16}$ in.) in collection of Mr. F. J. Martin Dent, London reproduced (reversed) in *The Idler* (May 1898) and as pl. 74 of *The Later Work of Aubrey Beardsley*.

but he was ready with a new show—a novel attraction. A glance through the old Casino programmes would give you a very considerable idea of his talent. What countless ballets, comedies, comedy-ballets, concerts, masques, charades, proverbs, pantomimes, tableaux-magiques, and peep-shows excentriques; what troupes of marionettes, what burlesques!

Ponchon had an astonishing flair for new talent, and many of the principal comedians and singers at the Queen's Theatre and Opera House had made their first appearance and reputation at the Casino.

This afternoon the pièce de resistance was a performance of Rossini's Stabat Mater, an adorable masterpiece. It was given in the beautiful Salle des Printemps Parfumés. Ah! what a stunning rendering of the delicious demodé pièce de décadence. There is a subtle quality about the music, like the unhealthy bloom upon wax fruit, that both orchestra and singer contrived to emphasize with consummate delicacy.

The Virgin was sung by Spiridion, that soft incomparable alto. A miraculous virgin, too, he made of her. To begin with, he dressed the rôle most effectively. His plump legs up to the feminine hips of him, were in very white stockings clocked with a false pink. He wore brown kid boots, buttoned to mid-calf, and his whorish thighs had thin scarlet garters round them. His jacket was cut like a jockey's, only the sleeves ended in manifold frills, and round the neck, and just upon the shoulders, there was a black cape. His hair, dyed green, was curled into ringlets, such as the smooth Madonnas of Morales are made lovely with, and fell over his high egg-shaped creamy forehead, and about his ears and cheeks and back.

The alto's face was fearful and wonderful—a dream face. The eyes were full and black, with puffy blue rimmed hemispheres beneath them, the cheeks, inclining to fatness, were powdered and dimpled, the mouth was purple and curved painfully, the chin tiny, and exquisitely modelled, the expression cruel and womanish. Heavens! how splendid he looked and sounded.

An exquisite piece of phrasing was accompanied with some curly gesture of the hand, some delightful undulation of the stomach, some nervous movement of the thigh, or glorious rising of the bosom.

The performance provoked enthusiasm—thunders of applause. Claude and Clair pelted the thing with roses, and carried him off in triumph to the tables. His costume was declared ravishing. The men almost pulled him to bits, and mouthed at his great quivering bottom! The little horses was quite forgotten for the moment.

Sup, the penetrating, burst through his silk fleshings, and thrust in bravely up to the hilt, whilst the alto's legs were feasted upon by Pudex, Cyril, Anquetin, and some others. Ballice, Corvo, Quadra, Senillé, Mellefont, Theodore, Le Vit, and Matta, all of the egoistic cult, stood and crouched round, saturating the lovers with warm douches.

Later in the afternoon, Venus and Tannhäuser paid a little visit to De La Pine's studio, as the Chevalier was very anxious to have his portrait painted. De La Pine's glory as a painter was hugely increased by his reputation as a fouteur, for ladies that had pleasant memories of him looked with a biassed eye upon his fêtes galantes merveilleuses, portraits and folies bergeres.

Yes, he was a bawdy creature, and his workshop a regular brothel. However, his great talent stood in no need of such meretricious and phallic support, and he was every whit as strong and facile with his brush as with his tool!

When Venus and the Chevalier entered his studio, he was standing amid a group of friends and connoisseurs who were liking his latest picture. It was a small canvas, one of his delightful morning pieces. Upon an Italian balcony stood a lady in a white frock, reading a letter. She wore brown stockings, straw-coloured petticoats, white shoes, and a Leghorn hat. Her hair was red and in a chignon. At her feet lay a tiny Japanese "Fanny," and upon the balustrade stood an open empty bird cage. The background was a stretch of Gallic country, clusters of trees cresting the ridges of low hills, a bit of river, a chateau, and the morning sky.

De La Pine hastened to kiss the moist and scented hand of Venus. Tannhäuser bowed profoundly and begged to have some pictures shown him. The gracious painter took him round his studio.

Cosmé was one of the party, for De La Pine just then was painting his portrait—a portrait, by the way, which promised to be a veritable chef d'œuvre, Cosmé was loved and admired by everybody. To begin with, he was pastmaster in his art, that fine, relevant art of coiffing; then he was really modest and obliging, and was only seen and heard when he was wanted. He was useful; he was decorative in his white apron, black mask, and silver suit; he was discreet.

The painter was giving Venus and Tannhäuser a little dinner that evening, and he insisted on Cosmé joining them. The barber vowed he would be de trop, and required a world of pressing before he would accept the invitation. Venus added her voice, and he consented.

Ah! what a delightful little partie carré it turned out. The painter was in purple and full dress, all tassels and grand folds. His hair magnificently curled, his heavy eyelids painted, his gestures large and romantic, he reminded one a little of Maurel playing Wolfram in the second act of the Opera of Wagner.

Venus was in a ravishing toilet and confection of Camille's, and looked like K****. Tannhäuser was dressed as a woman and looked like a Goddess. Cosmé sparkled with gold, bristled with ruffs, glittered with bright buttons, was painted, powdered, gorgeously bewigged, and looked like a marquis in a comic opera.

The salle à manger at De La Pine's was quite the prettiest that ever was.

AUBREY BEARDSLEY.

HERE THE MANUSCRIPT ENDS.

PREVIOUS EDITIONS OF
"THE STORY OF VENUS AND TANNHÄUSER"

"Under the Hill," *The Savoy*, vol. I, no. 1 (January 1896), pp. 151–170; vol. I, no. 2 (April 1896), pp. 187–196 [*The Savoy* version].

These two instalments constitute the first appearance of the text for Beardsley's "romantic story." Printed with the title "Under the Hill," this version utilised the names of "Helen," "the Abbé Fanfreluche" and "Mrs Marsuple" for "Venus," "Tannhäuser" and "Priapusa" respectively. In a heavily expurgated form the first number of *The Savoy* carried the plot through the early chapters of the original MS, while the second number offered a heavily censored version of Chapter VII with a lengthy footnote which corresponds to Chapter V. Five of Beardsley's illustrations, "The Chevalier Tannhäuser," "The Toilet of Venus" and "The Fruit Bearers" in the first issue and "St. Rose of Lima" and "Das Rheingold" in the second, were also included, although a promised sixth, "The Bacchanales of Sporion," never appeared. In addition, Beardsley's drawing of "A Footnote" was printed on the page immediately preceding the first instalment. Beardsley's illness prevented the next instalment, planned for *The Savoy*'s third number.

Under the Hill and Other Essays in Prose and Verse, London, 1904.

The first thirty two pages of this posthumous collection of Beardsley's prose constitute a reprint of *The Savoy* instalments, with the expurgations and altered names of the major characters strictly maintained. Brought out by John Lane, who contributed a prefatory publisher's note, this volume also includes "The Ballad of the Barber," "Carmen Ci" (a translation from Catullus), selections from Beardsley's table talk and two of his letters. Of the sixteen illustrations, five, "The Chevalier Tannhäuser," "The Toilet of Venus," "The Fruit Bearers," "St. Rose of Lima" and "Das Rheingold," come from *The Savoy* instalments of "Under the Hill."

The Story of Venus and Tannhäuser, London, 1907 [the Smithers version].

Printed "for private circulation" by Leonard Smithers, the publisher of *The Savoy*, this edition of Beardsley's novel was drawn from the original MS. It opened up all the cuts imposed by the censors and restored the leading characters to their appropriate names: Tannhäuser, Venus and Priapusa. It did not include, however, two sections from the second *Savoy* instalment which justify the presence of two drawings, "St. Rose of Lima" and "Das Rheingold," in the corpus of Tannhäuser illustrations, an omission minimised somewhat, at least, by the total absence of any Beardsley illustration from "the Smithers version." Smithers prefaced this volume with the following explanatory foreword:

> Only a portion of this work, Beardsley's most ambitious literary effort, has hitherto been printed, with the title "Under the Hill." The present work is a complete transcript of the whole of the manuscript originally projected by Beardsley. It has been deemed advisable, owing to the freedom of certain passages, to issue only a limited number of copies for the use of those literary students who are also admirers of Beardsley's wayward genius.

Only 300 copies of this 88 page volume were printed, 250 on hand-made paper and 50 on Japanese vellum.

The Story of Venus and Tannhäuser, New York, 1927.

As with "the Smithers version", this edition of Beardsley's fable is based upon the **original MS** and was "**Issued privately for subscribers only**" by N. L. Brown. The text is virtually identical to that appearing in Smithers's volume, although some printer's errors in the earlier imprint were corrected for this later version. This volume was swollen to 93 pages by the inclusion of six full page illustrations and ten headpieces, all drawn by Bertram R. Elliot. 750 copies were printed, all on hand-made Ingres paper.

Under the Hill or the Story of Venus and Tannhäuser, Paris, 1959.

This edition, published by Olympia Press, while claiming to be based upon the privately printed New York version of 1927, differs from it in several respects. Besides a series of alterations to both words and phrases, the two portions of *The Savoy* instalments, missing in the 1907 and 1927 imprints, were also restored. Beardsley's MS, with these modifications, appears on the first 71 pages, while pages 71 to 125 contain an attempt by a twentieth century Beardsley enthusiast, John Glassco, to complete the unfinished novel. Glassco also included nine of Beardsley's Tannhäuser drawings in the text: "Title page and frontispiece," "Venus," "The Chevalier Tannhäuser," "The Toilet of Venus," "The Fruit Bearers," "St. Rose of Lima," "Das Rheingold," "Venus between Terminal Gods" and the second version of "The Return of Tannhäuser."

SELECT BIBLIOGRAPHY

Thomas Beer, *The Mauve Decade*, New York, 1926.

Armand Bitoun, "Aubrey Beardsley et l'esthétisme homosexuel," *Les Lettres Nouvelles* (March/April 1967).

B. Brophy, *Black and White, a Portrait of Aubrey Beardsley*, London, 1968.

David Cecil, *Max*, London, 1964.

Alfred Douglas, *Oscar Wilde and Myself*, New York, 1914.

The Early Work of Aubrey Beardsley, London and New York, 1899.

Malcolm Easton, *Aubrey and the Dying Lady*, London, 1972.

Malcolm Easton, "Aubrey Beardsley and Julian Sampson: an Unrecorded Friendship," *Apollo* (January 1967).

R. Fry, "Aubrey Beardsley's Drawings," *Vision and Design*, London, 1924.

A. E. Gallatin, *Aubrey Beardsley, Catalogue of Drawings and Bibliography*, New York, 1945.

W. G. Good, "Aubrey Beardsley: a Reappraisal," *The Saturday Book*, Boston and Toronto, 1965.

D. J. Gordon, "Aubrey Beardsley at the V & A," *Encounter* (1966).

J. Gray (ed.), *Last Letters of Aubrey Beardsley*, London, 1904.

C. Gross, "'Soldier's Pay' and the Art of Aubrey Beardsley," *American Quarterly* (Spring 1967).

Rupert Hart-Davis (ed.), *The Letters of Oscar Wilde*, London, 1962.

Rupert Hart-Davis (ed.), *Max Beerbohm: Letters to Reggie Turner*, London, 1964.

R. Thurston Hopkins, "Aubrey Beardsley's School Days," *The Bookman* (March 1927).

A. W. King, *An Aubrey Beardsley Lecture*, London, 1924.

The Later Work of Aubrey Beardsley, London and New York, 1901.

Arthur H. Lawrence, "Mr. Aubrey Beardsley and His Work," *The Idler* (March 1897).

Henry Maas, J. L. Duncan, W. G. Good (eds.), *The Letters of Aubrey Beardsley*, London, 1971.

Haldane MacFall, *Aubrey Beardsley*, New York and London, 1928.

J. Lewis May, *John Lane and the Nineties*, London, 1936.

Nineteen Early Drawings by Aubrey Beardsley from the Collection of Harold Hartley, London, 1919.

Joseph Pennell, *Aubrey Beardsley and Other Men of the Nineties*, Philadelphia, 1924.

André Raffalovich (under pseudonym "Alexander Michaelson"), "Aubrey Beardsley," *Blackfriars* (October 1928).

André Raffalovich (under pseudonym "Alexander Michaelson"), "Aubrey Beardsley's Sister," *Blackfriars* (November 1928).

Brian Reade, *Aubrey Beardsley*, New York, 1967.

Brian Reade, *Aubrey Beardsley* (Victoria and Albert Museum exhibition catalogue), London, 1966.

Margery Ross (ed.), *Robert Ross: Friend of Friends*, London, 1952.

Robert Ross, *Aubrey Beardsley* (with revised iconography by Aymer Vallance), London, 1909.

Jack Smithers, *The Early Life and Vicissitudes of Jack Smithers*, London, 1939.

Arthur Symons, "Aubrey Beardsley," *The Fortnightly Review* (1898).

The Uncollected Work of Aubrey Beardsley, London and New York, 1925.

R. A. Walker (ed.), *A Beardsley Miscellany*, London, 1949.

R. A. Walker (ed.), *Letters from Aubrey Beardsley to Leonard Smithers*, London, 1937.

R. A. Walker (ed.), *Some Unknown Drawings of Aubrey Beardsley*, London, 1923.

Stanley Weintraub, *Beardsley*, London, 1967.

Edmund Wilson, "Late Violets from the Nineties," *The Shores of Light*, New York, 1952.